GRIM LOVERS 1
Lilith Leana

Table of Contents

Acknowledgement

A big thank you to my husband for always believing in me and never making me feel like I couldn't do it.

Cover art

Cover art from Depositphoto

Cover design

Lilith Leana with Canva

Brief Summary

The Beast

What if the Beast never turned into the Prince?

Belle and the Beast are married and live together, but Belle needs her Beast to take her in all the ways a husband should. She has devised a plan to seduce her husband.

The Beast is scared to hurt her, but Belle convinces him to take her.

Hook

What if Hook is the one to save Tinkerbell when she almost died due to lack of attention?

Tinkerbell almost died, but luckily Captain Hook was there to save her. She needs attention and physical contact to heal and restore her powers.

Hook finds Tinkerbell on the brink of death, and nurses her back to health. His touches help her, and excite her until neither can hold back the passion they feel for each other.

Frost

What if Jack Frost taught the Snow Queen to control her powers?

This story is a retelling of two classic tales that meet in the icy cold.

The Snow Queen gets help from Jack Frost to learn to control her powers. When the Snow Queen catches Jack pleasuring himself to an ice statue of her, it becomes steamy between them.

Jack Frost helps the Snow Queen control her powers, but he can't control his feelings for her anymore.

The Jungle Man

What if Tarzan found a dirty book while learning how to read with Jane?

Jane's feelings for Tarzan are starting to go beyond friendship, but she is holding herself back until Tarzan presents her with an offer she cannot refuse.

Tarzan has been drawn to Jane since he first saw her. She already has his heart, and now he also wants to give her his body.

Rumpelstiltskin

What if the Miller's daughter couldn't give away her firstborn to Rumpelstiltskin because it was already his?

The Miller's daughter has been cursed with powers to read people's minds. The King wants her to give him his deepest desire, but she can't find out what it is on her own.

Rumpelstiltskin will help the Miller's daughter at a price. His price becomes higher as the demands of the King increase, until he asks for something he cannot have.

READER ADVISORY: THIS story contains explicit sex scenes.

Grim Lovers 1 is a collection of five previously published standalone short erotic stories.

It is filled with your favorite fairytale retellings. Explicit sex scenes, standalone, no cheating or cliffhangers.

The Beast

What if the Beast never turned into the Prince?

I WAS MARRIED TO A Beast, and I loved every second of it. He was big, monstrous, hairy, and all mine. After we rid the village of Gaston and his toxic ideas, everyone accepted us as we were. We got married, and my father even walked me down the aisle, apologizing for everything he had done. Our union broke the curse on his servants, and we lived our married life in the castle.

I had everything I could dream of: a loving husband, a giant library, and amazing friends that weren't ceramics, but there was still one thing missing.

He had pleasured me plenty, but we hadn't gone all the way yet. My sweet Beast feared hurting me, but I needed my husband to fuck me raw. Teasing and flirting always ended in him pleasuring me. Not that I was complaining, but I had seen his monstrous cock and I wanted it to fill me up and stretch me to my limit.

So I devised a plan. All our staff would be gone for the evening, leaving us all alone in the grand castle. I would wear my most sexy lingerie, courtesy of Madame de la Grande Bouche. The food was ready and comprised all of his favorites, as well as some aphrodisiac food items. An automatic music player would play a seductive tune, another brilliant invention of my father. And to top it all off, I had locked all the doors and windows so he couldn't run.

I had just finished my bath, adding some rose scent to the water, to make me smell like his favorite flower. When I started to apply my body lotion, I could hear him enter the bathing room behind me. My Beast loved to watch me from a distance, not saying anything, just enjoying the view. I slowed my movements, lingering over every inch of my body, slowly rubbing the sweet-smelling lotion on my skin.

The arousal of the act excited me as I neared the sensitive tips of my breasts. My nipples puckered as I put a dab of lotion on each of them. I turned around so he could have a good view of my ministrations while I massaged both tips slowly and sensually. His labored breaths filled the small bathing room, and I knew he was getting turned on as well. A small moan escaped me when I pinched my nipples. He growled in response and a shiver of delight coursed through me. Would this be enough to finally break his resolve? To unleash the Beast and have him take me like a husband should take his wife?

I emitted another whimper as I kept stimulating my nipples. I could feel wetness gather between my legs. My arousal grew and the scent of it filled the air. He sniffed, and after I made another sound of desire, he was suddenly on me. His gigantic body covered my back, his arms surrounded me, and his hands roamed my body. He immediately went for my pleasure point. A guttural growl sounded from him as he discovered how wet and ready I was for him. He pushed a long and meaty finger inside of me, thrusting it in a maddening rhythm.

My muscles squeezed around his appendage as I gasped and moaned out in pleasure. His hungry growls in my ear only enhanced my arousal. He fucked me hard and fast with his finger, as I kept stimulating my breasts. I could feel the pleasure inside of me grow to incredible highs, and before I knew it, I crested the top of my climax.

I screamed as it engulfed me, my voice ricochet against the tiled walls. My body shivered, my muscles clenched around his finger, and he groaned behind me. I could feel his massive cock straining against his trousers at my back. I needed a moment to catch my breath, but I also needed his cock inside of me. Another moan escaped me as his finger left my pussy. Stretching my arm behind me, I tried grabbing him, but he evaded my grasp and left the bathing room before I got a hold of him.

My Beast left me as I was still shivering from the explosive orgasm he had just given me. Again, not taking his own pleasure, just providing me with mine. This would end tonight. His actions only made me more determined in my plan of seduction.

I quickly dressed in the gorgeous lingerie and evening gown that showed off all of my curves. It was the same golden color as the dress I had worn when we first danced. I put up my hair in an elegant updo, so my neck was available for him to kiss and nibble on. A shiver of anticipation filled me, and I rushed to the dining room. The climax had been amazing, but it had only fueled my arousal for him.

My Beast was already seated at the head of the table, looking at all the amazing food that was laid out. I gave him a quick peck on the lips and took my seat next to him.

"Dig in," I said, and gestured to all the delicious items before us.

Taking a duck leg, I started to feast on it, but my Beast remained silent beside me. I looked up and saw a frown grace his beautiful, monstrous face. I never grew tired of looking at him. His gorgeous tall horns, his soft brown fur, his cute black nose, and his bright blue eyes, all made the face of the husband I loved, unique.

"Where is the cutlery?" he asked.

I shrugged. "Probably all dirty. We will just have to eat with our hands."

He looked at me as I slowly licked the sauce off one of my fingers. His eyes turned hungry, fixated on my mouth. I opened my mouth, letting my tongue slide over my lips, wetting them. With a growl, he averted his eyes, focusing on the food before him. My husband attacked the meal with such enthusiasm that I watched him momentarily dumbstruck. He looked downright feral as he decimated the food. I had made him lose his control, but instead of taking it out on me sexually, he was taking his frustration on the way he ate.

When there were only scraps left, he whipped his face with a wet towel. A small laugh escaped me. In the time I had eaten one duck wing, he had devoured everything else. His eyes focused on me again. A low growl filled the room and a shiver of delight went through me.

"I'm ready for my dessert."

Before I could say anything, he had whipped his arm across the table, scattering the plates. He grabbed me and pulled me onto the table in front of him. I opened my legs, giving him access, and in one move, he ripped my panties off. I gasped, mourning the loss of the pretty little thing, but my gasp soon turned into a moan when his mouth was on me.

He devoured me with even more gusto than the meal. His massive tongue licked me, touching my entire pussy in one sweep. He opened my folds with his fingers, focusing his attention on my clit. My sounds of pleasure filled the empty dining room, mixed with the wet sounds of his mouth on my pussy.

"Please, fuck me," I begged, gripping his hair and pulling his head up.

He shook my hands loose and focused on his meal again. I wouldn't be ignored again.

"Please, fuck me, my husband. I need you to fill me with your cock."

He growled against my pussy, sending vibrations through me that only enhanced my pleasure. I was already so close to my climax, but I wanted him to come with me.

"Fill me, please."

He obeyed me, but not in the manner I had wanted. His tongue lapped at my clit as one of his thick fingers entered me. Pleasure filled me as my husband took care of my every need. He suckled and licked at my clit as he fucked me with his thick finger. When he curled the digit inside of me and touched my inner pleasure point, I almost shot off the table crying out in pleasure. The sensations were enough to set me off. Pleasure washed over me as my muscles squeezed around the delicious fullness that his finger created. A sound of satisfaction escaped me as pleasure filled my body, but my mind was not yet satisfied.

"Fuck me," I whispered, my voice hoarse from the loud sounds of desire I had emitted.

He pushed up from his chair and my heart leaped up in excitement, but he left me yet again. As if the devil was on his heels, my husband ran from the dining room, leaving me limp on the dining table.

As soon as my strength returned, I went to find him. There were only so many places he went to escape in our castle. I found him in the library, sitting in his big red chair. He was holding a book but looking into the fire, his mind someplace far away. I crawled into his lap, his warm embrace surrounding me.

"Is something wrong with me?" I asked, my voice barely audible over the crackling sound of the fireplace.

The question pulled him out of his thoughts. He looked at me with so much love and devotion in his eyes that it nearly took my breath away. He stroked my cheek with his finger, and I leaned into the touch.

"Of course not, my darling Belle. Why would you think that?"

"Then why won't you fuck me? I need you. I need my husband."

A deep and heavy sigh resounded from his chest, vibrating through me.

"I am afraid I will hurt you. Do I not please you enough? Are you not satisfied?" he asked, tracing my lips with his finger that still smelled like my desire.

"Of course I'm satisfied, but I want all of you."

He shook his head, pulling his hand back. I grabbed it before he could, desperate for his touch.

"I can give you everything that your heart desires, but I cannot give you that, my sweet wife."

"All I desire is you," I said, pulling his hand to my mouth, and sucking on his fingers, my taste mixed with his in a delicious cocktail. "I know that you won't hurt me," I said, switching fingers, sucking on them one by one.

A pained groan came from him. The fire in his eyes and the rock-hard erection beneath me spurred me on. Even if his mind told him he shouldn't, his body wanted me.

I pulled his hand down between us against my wet pussy. "Can't you feel how much I want you?"

He growled and pushed two fingers inside of me. I gasped at the intrusion, and his brows furrowed.

"You are too small," he growled, as he worked his fingers in my pussy.

"Give me more," I moaned.

He pushed a third meaty finger in, making me stretch in the most delicious way. My breathing came out in huffs, and I grabbed his arm to steady myself.

"You will never be able to take me," he said as he fucked me with his hand.

"Yes, I will," I moaned as I rode his fingers, chasing yet another orgasm. "You'll fit."

I grabbed his cock through his trousers, marveling at his size. He was substantially bigger than his three already-filling fingers, but I knew I could take him.

"Please fuck me, my beautiful Beast," I begged.

I pulled at the buttons of his trouser, but as soon as I freed him, he grabbed my hands. He pulled both high above my head, making my back arch. My breasts pushed into his face, and with a growl, he attacked my nipples. Pleasure rushed through me and I could do nothing to stop my climax from taking over. I moaned and begged my Beast, but he ignored my pleas and continued to pleasure me until my orgasm flushed my body. Waves of pleasure washed over me as I cried out my release. My whole body trembled, and I sank against him.

"Please, fuck me," I mumbled against his chest, absolutely exhausted by the triathlon of pleasure I had endured by his hands.

He gently hushed me as my eyes drooped close. I wanted to fight the sleep and make him fuck me, but my body decided otherwise. Dozing in his arms, he brought me to our bedroom. I fell asleep in the arms of my husband, thoroughly pleasured, but still not fucked.

I woke up in the middle of the night, determined to get what I wanted. I had to resort to Plan B, which I had prepared in case my carefully orchestrated seduction didn't work. Without waking my Beast, I tiptoed out of our bed. Grabbing the shackles I had stashed under it, I got to work securing him. A few times he almost roused, but luckily he kept on snoring like he usually did.

When he was fully detained by the bonds, I undressed and got rid of his undershorts. Finally, I had time to study his monstrous cock in peace. Even flaccid, it was massive and a little tinge of worry filled me. Maybe he was right and he would never fit me, but I pushed that thought out of my mind. He was my husband, and I was going to fulfill our marital bond tonight.

I studied his cock, loving the way it matched the rest of his monstrous appearance. It was dark, thick, and had ridges that would feel heavenly inside of me. Sitting between his legs, I leaned in to study it more closely. When my breath hit his hot skin, it started to stir. A small groan sounded from my Beast and I knew I had to act quickly before he woke up. I grabbed his cock gently, slowly stroking it up and down. It immediately started to grow in my hand, and soon I wasn't even able to encompass his girth with one hand. Using both my hands, I stroked him until he was fully erect. My Beast stirred again and moaned softly. I put my mouth on the mushroomed head, licking him and reveling in his manly taste.

With a start, he woke up. My Beast tried to get up, but the bonds held. He growled and looked at me, his eyes heavy with sleep. When he saw me naked on my knees, between his legs, working his cock he groaned. His cock jumped in my hand and I made a soft sound of surprise.

"What are you doing, my sweet Belle?" he asked, his voice rough with sleep and desire.

"Showing my husband that I can take him."

Before he could protest, I straddled him, positioning my pussy above his giant erection. It looked so much bigger between my legs. I glided my pussy over his enormous length, coating him in my wetness. He growled again, the sound only adding to my arousal.

"Fuck, Belle."

His voice sounded so tortured that I stopped. I looked up and gasped at the wild and feral look on his monstrous face. I had never seen him so on the edge of his control. It was magnificent; he was magnificent and all mine.

"I need you," I whimpered, as I pushed my pussy over his cock again.

He snarled, breaking the bonds and before I knew what was happening, he had me on my back on the bed.

"I'll give my wife what she needs," he growled.

He opened my legs and positioned his cock against my pussy. Very slowly, he pushed in. It felt like he would never fit as if he would just stretch me until I couldn't and he wouldn't even be inside yet. I moaned, and he growled, and after another push; he breached my entrance. The massive head of his cock was inside my pussy and I already felt stuffed. I looked down and moaned when I saw how much of him was left.

"You'll take all of me, won't you, my sweet Belle," he growled and pushed in deeper.

Words were lost to me, and I could only give him sounds of pleasure. He pushed, and I stretched as more and more of him filled me. It felt like he went on forever, but somehow my pussy could take it. Inch after delicious inch entered me and my body took it all. He touched nerve endings deep inside of me I didn't even know existed, sparking pleasure like never before. Just when I thought that there was no way that I could possibly take more of him, he bottomed out. A guttural groan sounded from him as his cock filled me all the way.

"Fuck, you're so tight," he hissed.

I moaned as I grabbed his arms, needing something to hold on to. As he pulled out, my eyes popped open and I let out the most guttural sound. I had almost forgotten about his ridges, but I felt every single one of them as they dragged along the inside of my pussy. He groaned, and I moaned as he pushed back in. My muscles squeezed around him, making the reentry harder and even tighter.

"You fit me like a glove," he said, his voice almost reverent.

I opened my eyes and looked into the beautiful eyes of my loving husband. It was almost as if a mirror was in front of me, reflecting every single emotion I felt. With every pull and every thrust, I could see the amazing pleasure we were both experiencing. It felt like coming home, so very comforting and pleasurable at the same time.

Pleasure inside of me sparked and when he bottomed out again after a particularly hard thrust, I suddenly came. The most unexpected orgasm washed over me, making my muscles squeeze around him as if to hold him inside of me forever. He snarled again and started fucking me hard. It almost felt like my orgasm didn't have an end, or maybe he just gave me a consecutive row of them. I didn't know, and I didn't care. All I could take think about was how good he felt inside of me and how my body was receiving pleasure in a way I could have never imagined.

I lost track of time, and of the times I came. I had unleashed the monster, and he was taking out all of his pent-up sexual aggression on me in the best of ways. My beautiful Beast was fucking me and it didn't seem like he would stop any time soon.

I glided on the waves of pleasure in the arms of my husband, reveling in all the sensations he was presenting me with. He made me reach highs I had never conquered before, going higher and higher until it almost felt like I was flying on a cloud of pleasure. When I was almost too sensitive to his never-ending fucking, he suddenly stilled, his cock throbbing deep inside of me. With a guttural groan, he released his seed, filling my pussy, and collapsed next to me. Both our breathing was coming out in huffs and pants, and I crawled into his arms.

He immediately turned to me, cradling my face and looking into my eyes with a searching gaze.

"Did I hurt you?" he asked, his voice rough with fatigue.

I shook my head, not trusting my voice, and crawled closer to him. He pulled me into his embrace and I fell asleep in the arms of my Beast that had thoroughly fucked my brains out.

THE END

Hook

What if Hook is the one to save Tinkerbell when she almost died due to lack of attention?

"EASY THERE, TINK," I heard a rough voice say.

I slowly blinked a few times. The spots dissipated from my view and I realized I was in the cabin of Hook. How did I get here? The last thing I remembered was... Peter kissing Wendy. I had felt my powers die out and had tried to warn Peter, but all he cared about was the new girl. Blinking again, I could make out a form in the small room. I squinted to try to focus, but that only hurt my head.

"Easy, girl," the voice said again.

I closed my eyes and let the voice soothe me. I felt, cherished and safe, things I hadn't felt in a long time. Even if it was thanks to Peter's nemesis, I didn't care. Hook had saved my life.

"Thank you," I said, my voice hoarse and faint.

"My pleasure," Hook said.

He sounded a lot closer than before. I carefully opened my eyes and saw him standing next to the bed I was lying on. His bed, in his cabin, on his ship. I should feel scared, being in the enemy's den, but I realized I wasn't.

Hook offered me a glass of water, and I drank it down greedily. It softened the burn in my parched throat. When he tipped the cup, his finger grazed my chin. A burst of desire shot through me and I moaned, making me choke on the water. He immediately took the cup away and dried me with a soft cloth.

"Please," I moaned.

"What do you need, my girl? Tell me and I will give it to you," Hook said.

His eyes were so warm and full of emotion that it warmed me from the inside. I hadn't really paid a lot of attention to his face until now. Every time we saw him or one of his Pirates, Peter always told us to run, and avoid any type of contact. I didn't understand the conflict between our people, but what I did know was that he was here with me, looking at me as if I was the best thing in Neverland.

Hook was handsome in a rugged way, almost the opposite of Peter's boyish good looks. His hair was a shiny black that looked so soft that my fingers itched to touch him. It was a bit too long, as was his facial hair, but it soothed him well. It gave his face a powerful look, and I couldn't look away.

"Touch," I whispered.

He gasped and his piercing blue eyes grew hot with desire.

"Are you sure? Because once I do I don't know if I can stop," Hook said.

I smiled and tried lifting my hand to caress his cheek, but I was still too weak.

"I trust you," I said.

He smiled, caressing my cheek so very softly. I could feel his touch vibrate through me, giving me back my powers.

"Don't you know that you should never trust a Pirate, my sweet girl?"

Hook leaned in and kissed me. I moaned into the kiss, opening my mouth. His lips felt chapped and hard underneath my soft ones. His face was weathered by the elements, as he was always outdoors working, not sitting inside on his ass. He growled in the kiss, plunging his tongue into my mouth, devouring me as he went. He tasted like all of my dreams come true, a real man, musky, tangy, and delicious. The kiss invigorated me, fueling my powers as I touched his tongue with mine.

We kissed as if we were the two only people in the world and it didn't matter that he was the Captain of the Pirates and I was the Fairy of the Lost Boys. I lost myself in the kiss and found the Fairy that I used to be. As the last of my kind, I felt like I had found a family again with the Lost Boys, but they never treated me like an equal. They always thought of me as Peter's annoying groupie. Hook was treating me like a woman for the first time in forever, and I loved every second of it.

It wasn't until he started caressing me that I realized how touch-starved I had been. His hand roamed my body, as his hook angled my face so he could conquer my mouth even more thoroughly. I arched into his touch, feeling every caress aiding my recovery. Soon I would be to my full strength again, but I didn't want to tell him because I never wanted this to end.

Hook broke off the kiss and we both gasped for air.

"Tell me I need to stop," Hook panted. His eyes searched mine for any sign of aversion.

"Never," I said, and grabbed his face, pulling it to mine again.

Our lips met, and the kiss was even hotter and more feral than the one before. The cool metal of his hook on my cheek was in stark contrast with his heated lips on top of mine. Even with a dangerous weapon so close to my face, his every touch ignited a fire inside of me that had been dormant for some time.

"Can I undress you?" Hook asked against my lips.

I moaned my consent, and with one sweep of his sharp appendage, he ripped my delicate green dress open. The soft fabric fluttered to the side and my breasts were exposed to the cool air in his cabin. My nipples puckered, begging for his touch. Hook pulled his head back and groaned when he looked at my naked form laying in his bed.

"You have no idea how long I have been dreaming of this," Hook said.

My breathing was coming out in huffs. "Probably as long as me."

His eyes shot to my face, and his brows furrowed. "But Pan?"

I shook my head. "We never did anything. I was more of an ornament for him than a person."

Hook growled and kissed my lips. "A fool he is, for he just lost his greatest treasure to a Pirate."

I wanted to answer, but when his lips descended to my neck, I lost the words I was going to say. I could only experience every sensation he was giving me with his mouth and tongue. The raspiness of his weathered lips combined with the soft slickness of his tongue made every touch magical. I was already at my usual power level, but each touch filled me with more strength. Arousal, desire, and pleasure rose inside of me, my body not used to it, but immediately welcoming it.

He sucked on my neck, creating goosebumps along my arms and moans in my throat. The tinge of pleasure and pain combined filled me with wonder. He licked the offended spot, and I made another sound of pleasure.

"You'll wear my mark for everyone to see," Hook whispered, as his mouth followed a path down my collarbone to my breasts.

I loved him marking me as his. It made me feel at home again, as if I belonged somewhere, to someone that cherished me. His lips reached the tips of my breasts and I moaned. His tongue switched between both nipples, wetting them. The cool air on the one was in stark contrast to his hot mouth on the other. He pleasured both breasts alternately and I could feel the arousal rise inside of me. My pussy got wet, and I needed more of his touch. I moaned and mewled with his every caress, lick, and nip. His mouth was doing things to me that overshot even my wildest fantasies.

"You taste like candy and fairy dust," Hook said between kisses.

He was the first man to taste me, so I would take his word on it. He licked me like I was the sweetest thing in the world, and he couldn't get enough of my taste.

"I might get addicted to it," Hook murmured against my breast.

A happy giggle bubbled out of me. This roguish Pirate, feared on all the seas, was getting addicted to my taste. His eyes shot up and I could see an amused twinkle in them. Not breaking eye contact, he licked my nipple again, slowly. My giggle turned into a moan as pleasure filled me.

His mouth descended over my stomach to my parted legs. Anticipation vibrated through me, as my pussy clenched around nothing, aching to be filled by him.

"I wonder if you're as sweet here," Hook said, as he swept his finger through my slick folds.

I gasped as he showed me the wetness coating his finger. When he licked it, I moaned at the same time as him.

"Even sweeter," he said, and dove between my legs.

I got no warning before his tongue suddenly plunged between my pussy lips. Pleasure shot through me as he licked every inch of me. His moans vibrated through me, only enhancing my pleasure. It was too much, too sensitive, too much pleasure. I tried closing my legs, but his massive shoulders blocked me. He hooked an arm around my leg, pinning me down on the bed. I totally surrendered to his ministrations, and I loved it.

Hook opened my folds with his hand as he licked me. Slowly, he stroked his metal prosthetic over my stomach, lower and lower until it was on top of my mound. The slight scratch left a soft red line on my skin. Another mark on my body that I would wear only for me to see. His hook was incredibly sharp and dangerous, but he handled it as if was an extension of his body that he had under his full control. The glistening weapon gently rubbed lower and lower until it touched my clit as he watched with reverent eyes.

The pleasure of his hand and tongue combined with the little tinge of pain from his hook was too much and I exploded in a cloud of pixie dust. Waves and waves of pleasure washed over me as my body trembled, my wings fluttered and fairy dust covered us both. Hook held me, murmuring sweet words as I got down off my amazing high. His dangerous metal claw was positioned next to my body, no longer touching my sensitive clit.

"Good girl," Hook said.

Those words did something inside of me. His praise of my first orgasm beneath his hands was almost as arousing as his touches had been. I moaned and I could feel another climax rising already. I wanted to explain it or beg him to give me another, but I couldn't find the right words. Hook looked at me and I saw understanding in his bright blue eyes.

"You're going to come for me again and again, like the good girl you are."

I moaned and nodded. His mouth descends on my pussy again. He licked me as he pushed a finger inside of me. I clenched around him, moaning as he gave me more and more pleasure. His soft tongue laved my sensitive clit, soothing it and pleasuring it at the same time. He added another finger inside of me, thrusting at a leisurely pace. He slowly built up my orgasm, making me aware of it and when it would crest.

"Are you ready for the next one, my sweet girl?" Hook asked.

After I gave a sharp nod, he added a third finger, slowly stretching me to take it.

"You're so tight. You'll feel amazing wrapped around my cock," Hook said.

When I was able to take all three of his fingers, he started a steady pace of thrusting. He stretched and filled me just right, fucking me with his fingers in a way that made my climax gently rise inside of me. When he lapped at my clit again, the pleasure almost reached its climax, but he held his fingers motionless inside of me. I moaned and wiggled, trying to get him to move again, but he held his hand still.

After another delicious lick, Hook lifted his head and said. "You're going to fuck yourself on my fingers, chasing your orgasm, and you're going to come for me."

My mouth fell open in shock, and my muscles clenched around his fingers. He groaned, dove down again, and started licking my clit with those delicious little movements. The pleasure rose inside me again, but I needed more friction to be able to reach it.

"Please, Hook," I begged, but he held his hand still.

With a huff, I started to move my hips, fucking myself on his hand. I closed my eyes and tried to surrender to the feeling, but it didn't work.

"Look at me," Hook murmured against my clit, the words vibrating through me.

A shiver of delight filled me, and I opened my eyes. His encouraging gaze helped me find my confidence. I moaned and moved my hips as he lapped at my clit. The friction was amazing as his tongue worked my clit. The balled-up tension inside of me was released, and pleasure washed over me. My muscles clenched around his fingers, only enhancing the amazing feeling of being filled by him and I came with a pleasured cry. Pixie dust surrounded us again, the gold specks giving his skin a warm undertone. He growled, and the vibrations only prolonged my climax. Pleasure filled my every sense as my whole body released the tension it had built up.

He dragged his fingers out, licking my release and pixie dust from his hand.

"You did amazing," Hook said between licking his fingers. He looked at me and added. "Good girl."

Another shiver washed over my body, filled with the same pleasure as my orgasm.

"How are you feeling?" Hook asked.

I sighed. How to even describe the turmoil that was waging war inside of me? Amazing, invigorated, powerful?

"Better," I said, going for the easy answer instead of the existential one.

"Ready for another?"

With a moan, I nodded. I was ready for everything he was willing to give me. He stood up from the bed and undressed with hurried hands. His body was amazing, muscular, hairy, and manly, and for this brief moment in time, all mine. His cock rose proudly between his legs, mouthwatering large. He gripped it, stroking it a few times.

I could see a bead of precum on the tip and couldn't resist my urge to taste him. I sat up in the bed, grabbed his cock, and pulled him to me. With a startled groan, he let me. His cock felt hard beneath my touch, but his skin was soft. I leaned over and swept my tongue over the head of his cock. His musky, salty taste exploded in my mouth, and I moaned in delight. With a groan, he pulled me off him.

"I don't want this to end too soon," Hook managed to say between gritted teeth.

I didn't want this to end ever, but I didn't want to scare him off, so I remained silent and released his cock from my grip. Now that I was sitting upright, I could stretch my wings. I opened them and his gaze drifted to them.

"You're beautiful," Hook said with an almost reverent tone.

I could feel my cheeks heat up and my wings fluttered in excitement. With every flap, the pixie dust I had created whirled around the cabin. Soon, every inch of his personal space would be covered in the stuff. Peter always hated it when I left a trail of fairy dust, but Hook didn't seem to mind.

He pushed me down on the bed, leaning over me. My wing stuck underneath me at an awkward angle and I winced. He immediately pulled back and analyzed the situation. Stroking his bearded chin in a move that shouldn't be as sexy as it was, he shook his head.

"What position will be comfortable for you?"

I didn't know. I never had sex with a non-fairy before, and all my fairy experience was so long ago, I didn't remember much of it. When he saw the dumbfounded look on my face, he smiled gently at me.

"No worries, we'll figure it out."

Hook looked around his small cabin and pulled his chair in the middle of the room. He sat on it and spread his arms wide, inviting me to sit down on his lap. I bit my lip, admiring his powerful legs that lead my gaze to his hard cock. When I hesitated for a moment too long, he growled. The low and deep sound vibrated through me and I moaned in response.

"Are you going to be a good girl and sit on my lap?"

My wings fluttered, and I flew to him, my feet never touching the ground. I landed on his lap. His hands immediately encompassed my waist as he pulled me on top of his cock. I was still soaking wet from my previous orgasms, and his massive cock slipped easily into my waiting entrance. I moaned when he stretched me more than his three fingers had done at the same time as Hook let out a muttered curse.

"Good girl," Hook managed to get out.

His encouraging words were enough to let me break free from my internal struggles. He wanted me as much as I wanted him. His rock hard cock was deep inside of me, and I was going to make sure that this was as enjoyable for him as it was for me. I squeezed my inner muscles as I pushed up, gripping his cock hard with my pussy. As I descended again, I gripped his hand and put it on my breast. I gripped his faux hand to steady myself as I rode his cock.

"Fuck, you're marvelous Tink," he said.

"You feel so good inside of me, Hook," I moaned.

I lifted his hook to my lips, as my wings, and hips worked to ride him hard. His eyes were fixated on my mouth, as I slowly licked his metal appendage. He groaned and pulled me into his arms to kiss me. His mouth devoured mine as he pushed his hips up to fuck me harder.

My climax rose with each thrust. The pleasure inside of me getting bigger and bigger. I pulled back, panting to look at Hook's expressive face, which only enhanced my arousal. His bright blue eyes were hot with desire, and his face was contorted with pleasure. I wanted him to lose control inside of me. I needed him to claim me as his forever.

"Please," I moaned, not entirely sure what I was begging for.

"You're going to come and squeeze me hard like a good girl, aren't you?"

I nodded, riding him harder, chasing that high together with him.

"You're going to make me come as well. I'm going to fill your good girl cunt with my seed. Making you all dirty and ruining you for any other man. You're mine, Tink."

His dirty words were enough to push me over the edge. I screamed out his name as my orgasm washed over me. Pleasure filled my body as I trembled on top of him, my muscles squeezing his rock-hard cock. I could feel him throb inside of me, and with another thrust and a pleasured cry, he came as well. My pussy milked his cock as he filled me with his seed. My wings fluttered and a massive burst of pixie dust coated us and the cabin in a golden layer.

I let myself fall against his chest, and immediately his arms surrounded me. His hand caressed my quivering back, and he whispered soothing words in my ear.

"You did so well, my good girl."

Another shiver of delight went through me at hearing his praise. I wanted to stay like this forever, warm, sated, safe, and cherished.

A loud knock on the door startled us.

"Uhm, Captain," a voice said through the door. "Pan is here, and he isn't looking happy."

I shivered again and nestled closer to Hook. A million thoughts crossed my mind, but one remained firmly in place. I wanted to stay here with Hook.

He growled and his embrace tightened. "Tell him we're busy. Tink is staying here. She almost died because of him, and I won't let that happen again."

There was silence on the other side of the door and then heavy footsteps that walked away. I looked up at him. My savior, the Captain of the Pirates, my Hook.

"Are you sure?" I asked, my voice thick and unsteady.

He gently cupped my face with his hand and stroked my cheek with his hook. "I have never been more sure of anything in my whole life. Do you want to stay? I can always drop you off somewhere safe by the mermaids, or wherever you..."

I cut off whatever foolish thing he was about to say next with a kiss. His hard mouth softened under mine, and he kissed me back. I didn't know what the future would hold for us, but I knew how he made me feel, and that was all that mattered.

THE END

Frost

What if Jack Frost taught the Snow Queen to control her powers?

"AGAIN," JACK SAID.

I huffed out an annoyed breath but listened to him and created yet another ice statue of him. I was forever grateful that he had come to the castle just in time to help me and prevent a forever winter in my country, but his training techniques were a bit... self-centered.

Since the beginning of our training, I have created a thousand statues of him, a million snowflakes shaped like his head, a mirage in the sky of him on a horse, and even an ice castle. He also thought me a dozen different ways to harness my power and control my emotions, but it was almost like he was testing and poking me to see when I would crack under his constant pestering.

"Again," Jack said.

A little mischievous idea entered my thought. The next statue I created of him had a slightly bigger nose. The next one had frizzy hair, and the one after that had short legs. It took five more statues of him looking more and more grotesque before he caught on.

He crossed his arms, with his little smirk forever plastered on his face. "You think that's funny?"

I giggled as the next statue I created mirrored his stance, but had stick arms. Jack shook his head, trying to hide his smile but failing miserably.

He rolled up his sleeves, showing off his muscular arms. He wasn't massively built, but he had muscles all over, and when he showed them off I suddenly had a hard time concentrating on things.

"Two can play that game," Jack said and created five statues with one flick of his hand.

I still marveled at his powers. He had taught me so much, but he had decades of practice before me. When I inspected the statues, I noticed they were of both of us, depicting increasingly erotic positions. I gasped and turned to him. He shot me a challenging look with one eyebrow arched. He was trying to get under my skin, and it was working, but I couldn't admit that. I was still a queen, and I wouldn't let him embarrass me. We were both adults. It just happened that I had a crush on him, and those images were creating fantasies in my head about what it would be between us.

I took a deep breath, and worked on creating a life-like statue of him, as detailed as I could. I filled in some things I hadn't seen yet, like his muscles, and six-pack, but the moment supreme would be his cock. I gave him the smallest cock I could think of.

Jack's first look was one of appreciation as he saw the attention to detail I had put into it, but when he got to his appendage, his eyes shot hot with fire. He flicked his hand and let it grow to a size I knew couldn't be real, but I watched transfixed anyway.

"This is more accurate," he said gesturing to it.

I laughed. "No way."

Suddenly, he was standing before me, almost touching. He was as tall as me, and his mouth was level with mine. I wanted to kiss him, but I wouldn't be the one to make the first move.

"Do you want me to show you?" Jack asked.

His cocky grin was nowhere to be seen, his face suddenly more serious than I had ever seen before. I wasn't sure what to say, but my dear sister that was yelling at me disrupted my answer.

"You gotta come see this." She stopped when she saw us so close together, a cute blush on her face from the running. "Oh. Am I interrupting something?"

Her husband ran after her, and I immediately took a step back. If they were both here, it must be something important.

I nodded at Jack and said. "We'll continue our training later."

His charming grin was plastered on his face again and he gestured to the castle on the mountain behind him. "You know where to find me."

After I dealt with my state affairs, which were not nearly as urgent as my sister had led me to believe, I went back to Jack's castle. I wanted to discuss what had happened earlier. There was a definite chemistry between us, but we shouldn't act on it. He was my instructor, and I was queen. It would never work, especially considering he would leave as soon as I had mastered my powers fully.

When I reached his room, I heard strange noises coming from behind the door. It almost sounded as if he was in pain. I opened the door and saw him standing in the middle of the room, stroking his cock in front of a statue of me, naked on my knees.

With a gasp, I drew his attention, and he cursed. With a flick of his hand, the statue disappeared and suddenly he was standing before me, absolutely naked, nothing obstructing my view. I could see that his actual cock was as life-like as the one on the statue I had created. He was absolutely magnificent. His whole body was lean, and muscular without even a speck of hair, and his pale cock was massive and fully erect in his hand. With another flick of his hand, he created a garment, but before it could hit his skin, I dissolved it into snowflakes.

"Don't," I said, my voice echoing against the ice walls.

Jack pulled his hand from his cock as I took a step closer.

"Stop," I said and he froze.

I slowly got down on my knees and repeated myself more clearly.

"Don't stop."

Kneeling before him, I let my clothes disappear. Jack gasped and looked at me with wide eyes. His heated gaze roved my body and I could feel my nipples pucker.

"Don't stop with what you were doing," I said and gestured my head towards his hard cock.

As if not sure, he slowly gripped his cock again. A tremble went through his whole body as he pumped his cock with lazy strokes while looking at my naked body.

"Is this what you were fantasizing about?" I asked, while I spread my thighs so he could see my pussy.

A tortured groan erupted from his throat as he worked his erection harder. Arousal grew inside of me as I watched his hand move over his delicious cock. I let the icy floor move like a carpet, so he slid closer to me. His cock looked even better in close up. I could see every vein running along his length and I was dying to taste it.

"Don't stop," I said again.

Jack stroked his erection while looking at me with fire in his eyes. He made sounds of pleasure but didn't speak a word. I had never seen him so quiet before. Now I knew what the trick was to shut him up. A smirk lifted my mouth, and he moaned.

"Are you going to come all over my breasts?" I asked as I cupped them.

My nipples puckered when his heated gaze fixated on them. The cold never bothered me, but his hot looks did things to my body that I hadn't felt in a long time. I pinched my nipples between my fingers and bit my lip to stifle my moan.

Jack cursed and worked his cock faster. I could see his body tremble and tense. His sharp inhales of breath were the only warming I got before he came. His seed shot out and covered my naked chest as he groaned. It felt pleasantly cool on my skin. I had expected it to be warm, but it matched his body temperature as it did mine.

"Do you feel better?" I asked.

He groaned and pulled me into an embrace, not caring that it got his seed on his chest as well.

"Fuck, that was hot," Jack said.

His body trembled, as he hugged me close, his face buried in my hair.

A giggle escaped me. "I would rather say cold, but..."

My words were caught off when he captured my mouth with his. The kiss was filled with longing and pent-up desire. This kiss was going to be the beginning of the evening, I wanted him so much. I knew it wasn't smart and that there were a thousand good reasons to not do this, but the one that overruled it all was that I needed him. I may be a queen and ruler of a country, but I was also a woman with needs that I knew only Jack could fulfill.

With a flick of his hand, Jack created a massive throne suited for a queen. It was beautiful with snowflakes and crystals adorning the backrest, and soft, glimmering pillows of snow on the seat. He gently pushed me down on it and kneeled before me.

"My turn," he said and dove in between my legs.

A gasp escaped me as his amazing mouth attacked my pussy. It felt like he was determined to give me the same amount of pleasure he had experienced. His lips and tongue felt divine against my skin, his temperature matching mine.

"Oh Jack, that feels good," I moaned as he circled my clit with his tongue.

"Fuck, you're delicious," he murmured against my pussy.

I gripped the armrests for balance while the arousal inside of me grew. It was incredibly hot to see Jack, my teacher, kneeling between my legs, determined to give me pleasure. As he pulled back, I mewled in disappointment. His cheeky grin was back on his face and I loved the twinkle in his eyes.

"Are you ready for more?" Jack asked.

I just nodded, not sure what more he could give me than the pleasure of his mouth. His mischievous grin turned wider and with a flick of his hand, he created something out of ice. My eyes widened when I realized it was a glistening dildo. It was almost a perfect match for his cock, but two sizes smaller.

"I'm going to work this in you slowly and let it grow until you're ready to take me," Jack said.

Before my eyes, the dildo grew until it was the same size as him. My eyes shot from the dildo to his face to his cock and back. My muscles clenched around nothing and I moaned in need.

"Fuck, yes, please Jack," I moaned.

"Is my Snow Queen begging for my cock?" he asked with his head cocked to the side.

I huffed out an annoyed breath, sitting up straighter, ready to close my legs. His hand stopped me, pressing my legs wide as he came closer. He sat so close that I couldn't close my legs, his shoulders blocking me.

"A queen doesn't beg," I said breathlessly.

"But it look so good on you," he said with a smirk.

He teased the dildo between my pussy lips, coating it in my juices. I moaned as the cold temperature hit me. It was a tinge colder than him, which created an amazing sensation in my pussy. A tremble went through my body as my arousal grew.

"Are you ready to beg?"

I shook my head as he pulled the dildo back up, showing me how wet it had gotten from my juices. He let it decrease in size and licked it.

"I could get addicted to your taste," Jack said.

Before I could answer, he pushed the dildo inside. Even the smaller size, already felt big and stretched me in a delicious way. I moaned as he pushed more and more inside, stuffing me with his icy appendage.

"Are you going to take my cock as well as this?" Jack asked as the dildo finally bottomed out inside.

I could feel his fingers graze against my clit as he pulled back and pushed it inside of me again. My pleasure grew with each thrust of the dildo and each caress on my clit. I couldn't answer his question as I was so caught up in the sensations he was giving me.

"Are you ready for more?" Jack asked as he kept pleasuring me.

"More," I moaned, nodding and spreading my legs wider.

My muscles squeezed around the dildo as it increased in size, making me feel fuller than before. He thrust it in and out, each stroke sparking pleasure inside of me.

"More," I moaned again, knowing he was still bigger.

He growled, and let the dildo grow again. He fucked me harder with it, his eyes focused on my face.

"Jack, please," I said.

He leaned closer to me, eyes focused on me, thrusting the enormous dildo inside of me.

"Tell me what you need and I'll give it to you."

I was so close to my orgasm that it was hard to form thoughts, but I knew I just needed a little push to get me there.

"Clit," I gasped out.

Immediately he leaned over and put his mouth on my pussy. He sucked on my clit as he kept thrusting inside of me, and pleasure washed over me. With a pleasured cry, I found the release that had been building up inside of me. My body trembled as my muscles squeezed around the dildo, gripping it tight. Jack growled against my clit, the vibrations only enhancing my pleasure. Wave after wave of pleasure filled my senses.

I let myself fall back onto the throne, little trembles still racking over my body. I gently pushed Jack's head away when it became too much. He gave me a last lingering lick as he pulled back. After he pulled the dildo out, he licked my juices off it. I moaned at the erotic image he was presenting sucking on the dildo that looked just like his cock.

"Ready for the real deal?" he asked with a wink as he let the dildo disappear with a flick of his hand.

"Yes," I said and transformed the throne into a massive bed.

I crawled to the middle of the silky, icy sheets and motioned him to come to join me. Jack jumped up on the bed, gave another hop, and nodded approvingly.

"Nice bounce," he said as he touched the sheets. "Great quality."

I pulled him on top of me before he could ask about the thread count on the magic snow sheets I had created.

"Less talking, more fucking," I said before I kissed him.

His tongue met mine in an explosive kiss that only stoked my arousal again. His body slid over mine, and I could feel my hard nipples against his soft chest. I wrapped my legs around him and grabbed his shoulders to pull him close to me. His hard cock nestled against my pussy and I moaned at the contact.

"Inside of me. Now," I said in between kisses.

He moaned in answer and positioned his cock at my entrance. With one thrust he sunk inside of me, stretching me and filling me to my limit. Luckily he had prepped me with the dildo, or it might not have been possible to fit him in one go. Our pleasured sounds mingled and echoed in the icy castle.

"Fuck, you feel amazing," he groaned.

"You too," I moaned in response.

After that our words were lost when our bodies and souls connected on a deeper level. Jack fucked me hard, each thrust creating more and more pleasure. The pleasure he was giving me felt like it would be too much. I knew this was too good to ever walk away from. His eyes were filled with so many emotions it was hard to sift through, but I hoped to recognize the same things I felt for him.

This connection we had went further than just amazing sex and compatible temperature. Jack was a friend, a teacher, and a confidant for me in a way I never had. He understood me, and my powers and all that came with them. Without him I would have been lost, alone, cast away by my people. My sister loved me, but she could never understand what it was like to live with the fear of hurting the people around you. With Jack, I didn't have that fear. Whatever ice or snow magic I threw at him, he could take it, deflect it or use it. He made me feel safe. If I ever lost him...

"Hey, beautiful", he said and stroked my cheek softly. "I'm here. Focus on me."

He thrust into me again, grounding me with him. Jack had realized that I had gone to a dark place in my mind, and had pulled me back to him.

"Yes, you're here," I said. "So fuck me."

"As long as you need me."

His words felt like it had a double meaning. I knew, I think I would need him forever. But I couldn't say that. Not yet. Not now. I banned the dark thoughts from my mind and focused on us again. His amazing cock slid through the folds of my pussy again and again. It wouldn't be long before I would come again and I wanted him to join me.

"Please, Jack," I moaned as I squeezed my muscles around him.

Jack let out a strangled groan as he fucked me faster. "What do you need?"

"You," I said. "I need to feel you come inside of me."

With a curse, he pummeled me harder. He slid his hand between us, stroking over my clit, starting my orgasm. A hoarse cry of pleasure came from me as he pushed me hard into the bed, fucking me as if his life depended on it. A moment later I could feel his body tremble and his cock throb inside of me. With a strangled groan he came and filled me with his seed. Waves of pleasure washed over me as my muscles milked the last of his release with our joined orgasm.

With a gasp, he pulled out, and let himself fall next to me. He pulled me close to him, stroking my hair with shaking hands. After we caught our breath, we kissed lazily, enjoying the feel of each other's bodies close together.

"What if I stayed?" Jack asked, his voice, light and airy, but the question felt heavy in the air.

"What do you mean?" I asked, turning my face to him.

He evaded my eyes and played with a lock of my hair.

"You're already almost as powerful as me and soon I can't teach you more. But what if I stayed anyway."

He still wasn't looking at me, but his words and actions made something warm inside of me.

"Why?" I asked, hoping for an answer that would reveal his true feelings for me.

"To be by your side, if you'll have me." When I didn't answer immediately, Jack laughed and shook his head. "Forget I said that. I didn't..."

I broke off his answer with a kiss. This was even better than I had dreamed of.

"I would love that," I said.

We made love the rest of the night. Jack stayed by my side as an advisory to the throne and later as my husband.

THE END

The Jungle Man

What if Tarzan found a dirty book while learning how to read with Jane?

"HI JANE," TARZAN SAID and I turned around with a smile.

We had been in the jungle for a few weeks now and his language skills had really skyrocketed. He had read almost every book we had in camp twice. When I realized what was in his hand, I knew it would change our friendship forever.

"What is this?" he asked as he held up a magazine with a nude woman on the cover.

I almost choked on my tea. Tarzan helpfully patted my back as I coughed, while trying to regain my composure. Of course, I knew what it was, but I wasn't ready to have that type of conversation with Tarzan. I developed feelings for him, and it was easier to be friends with him than try to take that to the next level. I made a move to get the papers he was holding, but he was much quicker and more powerful than me.

Tarzan cocked his head, looking at me with a calculating gaze. "You always say that books contain knowledge and the truth. I want you to teach me about what is in this book."

"That isn't a book," I tried, but I knew it wouldn't work on him.

For growing up in the jungle and having only learned about the human world a few weeks ago, he was a remarkably intelligent man.

"Don't," Tarzan said and shook his head. "Don't talk to me like I don't know what is a book and isn't."

He opened the magazine, and I saw a flash of breasts and a lot of naked skin. Silently, I cursed my father for bringing something like that along on our trip, but I couldn't blame him. I averted my eyes, but they drifted to his loincloth, which was looking more filled out than usual. God, I loved looking at him, and I couldn't tear my eyes away. He was always showing off so much skin that I was almost used to it, but I still marveled at his muscular physique.

"I want you to teach me about mating. I have seen the animals in the jungle do it, but I want to know how humans do it."

"Sex," I blurted out.

Tarzan looked at me with a raised eyebrow. "Sex?"

God, why did it sound even more decadent on his lips? I swallowed, gathered my strength, and nodded. "It's called sex between people."

"Can I sex you, Jane?" Tarzan asked as he stepped closer to me.

It was suddenly hard to breathe, as his muscular chest was level with my face, and I imagined licking his skin and all kinds of dirty scenarios.

"It is. Can I have sex with you?" I said with a breathless voice.

Tarzan grabbed my hips and pulled me against his hardening cock. "Yes," he growled.

"Oh, no, no. I didn't mean it like that," I said as I pushed my hands against his chest.

As the palms of my hands touched his naked skin, I suddenly forgot why I wanted to push him away. His manly, musky scent surrounded me. He smelled like the jungle, sweat, and man, a delicious cocktail that took my breath away. His chest felt so good beneath my fingertips, and I wondered how the rest of him would feel. I needed to breathe, and I needed to think and I couldn't do that while plastered against his body. I took a step back as I tried to calm my breathing.

"I know how to give myself pleasure," Tarzan said as his hand disappeared beneath his loincloth. "I want you to teach me how to give you the same pleasure."

His voice sounded rougher than usual as he stroked his cock beneath his loincloth. I should tell him to stop, should explain proper etiquette, and teach him it isn't respectable, but I was too fascinated by his movements. Growing up, I went to an all-girls boarding school. I knew the mechanisms and the basics of sex, but I have never experienced it for myself. I'd never even seen a cock before, and now there was this gorgeous male, stroking his in front of me. If only, I was a stronger woman, I could tell him to stop, but I wasn't.

"Show me," I said, voice breathless and my eyes focused on the movements beneath the fabric.

"Then you'll teach me?" Tarzan asked, stopping his movements.

I almost whimpered, but I nodded. I really shouldn't, but I wanted to.

"Say it, Jane," Tarzan said, and lifted a finger to my chin, tilting my head higher so I looked into his gorgeous, intensely piercing eyes. They were hot with a burning intensity that made me gasp. "Say that you'll teach me how to pleasure you and how to have sex with you."

Oh God, he really was going to make me spell it out. It shouldn't be as arousing as it was. He grasped my chin and caressed my bottom lip with his thumb. A shiver of desire went through me, and I could feel myself getting wet.

"I'll teach you," I said. "But we need to go somewhere private."

We were standing in the middle of the camp, and I didn't want my father walking in on us pleasuring each other. He nodded, and before I could suggest a location, he grabbed me and ran from the camp. The jungle whooshed by, as he ran with me in his arms, and swung from vine to vine. One powerful arm surrounded me, and the other used the vines and tree branches to get us higher and higher. I was plastered to his muscular chest and loved the feel of his skin against mine. His scent and warmth surrounded me, and I closed my eyes, reveling in the experience of Tarzan. It still amazed me how strong and fast he was, as he effortlessly took us to the top of the highest tree.

Before I knew it, I had to let go of him, and we were standing on the top of a tree overlooking the Jungle. The view never ceased to inspire me. I wanted to draw every corner and every vantage point of it, but it would take a lifetime to do it. When Tarzan took my hand and turned me to him, I forgot all about drawing and focused on the man before me.

He gestured for me to sit on a protruding branch as he stood before me. When I sat, he ripped off his loincloth, and I gasped. His cock was marvelous, but before I could take a good look, he grabbed it and started caressing it with urgent movements.

"Wait," I said, and he stopped. "Come closer and show me."

Tarzan gripped his erection tight and stepped closer. His cock was as magnificent as the rest of him. Massive, hard, and powerful. His hand trembled as if trying to control his urge to make quick work of his pleasure. A bead of fluid adorned his tip, and I had the undeniable urge to lick it, but that wouldn't be proper. None of the thoughts that raced through my mind were proper.

"Show me how you pleasure yourself," I said.

He grunted and started to stroke himself again, slower this time, so I could study his movements. His grip on his cock was so tight that I could see the skin move slightly with each pull. It stretched and I could see his veins running along his length. As he stroked downwards, the stretch on the skin was reversed, and I could see the head of his cock appear. There was more fluid coming from it now, slicking his movements, as he pushed over the head each time before he went down again.

The motions were rhythmical and mesmerizing. His balls swung low, almost like a pendulum. Every so slowly, he increased in speed until he was pulling on his cock harshly. His breathing sped up and his grunts deepened. The sounds he was making made a shiver run along my spine, down inside of me until it nestled just above my pussy. I could feel my inner muscles clench, and wetness seep out, as I bit my lip, trying to stifle my own moans. This was the most arousing thing I had ever seen, and I couldn't tear my eyes off Tarzan.

I looked up at his face, and I could see it contorted in pleasure. His mouth was open so he could breathe and grunt freely as his eyes were firmly fixed on me. I could almost feel the lust radiate from them, coursing through me.

"Can I splash on you?" Tarzan asked.

I gasped, never imagining receiving such a question. "Yes, please," I said without thinking.

He grunted, taking a step closer until his cock was almost in my face. "I will pleasure myself all over your face," he said as he stroked his cock faster until it was almost vibrating.

I should correct his language, but it was somehow even hotter how he expressed himself in his own way.

"Jane," he grunted, and that was the only warning I got before he came.

The first rope of cum shooting out, hit me on the chin, the second on my breasts, and the rest trickled out as he kept stroking himself. His moans of pleasure vibrated through me as I could see his cock pulse, pushing out the last of his seed. His scent had turned muskier, and earthier when he had released himself.

Tarzan released his cock with a satisfied grunt as he looked at my face. I must look ridiculous with his cum on my chin, dripping off. He immediately grabbed his loincloth and gently brushed it over the spots he had come on.

"Thank you," I said.

I wasn't sure if I meant the showing or the gentle cleanup. Either way, I loved how free Tarzan was with his body, mind, and touch. He dropped the loincloth on the tree and cupped my chin. I was hoping for a kiss, but after staring at my mouth intently, he released me with another grunt.

"Thank you, Jane, for letting me pleasure myself on you." Tarzan sat down and gestured eagerly at my pussy. "Now you show."

Oh boy, was I really going to do this? His display of pleasure aroused me, and I wouldn't mind a release myself, but actually opening my legs to show him, was way out of my comfort zone. He noticed my discomfort and scooted closer to his knees. Touching my knee, he rubbed his thumb over the fabric, searching for something in my eyes.

"You don't have to if you don't want to, Jane."

Those comforting words were enough to make me decide. It was only fair for me to show him what he had shown me. After a deep steadying breath, I smiled at him, gripping his hand for support.

"I want to, Tarzan."

With a reassuring nod, I gently pushed his hand off my knee and opened my legs. His eyes focused on my movements, as I slowly pulled the thin fabric of my skirt higher and higher until I was revealing my panties.

"You're wet," Tarzan murmured as he saw the dark patch in the center of my panties.

I moaned and nodded. "I get wet when I'm aroused, and watching you was very arousing."

He leaned forward, almost touching, and took in a deep breath. "Smelling you is arousing," Tarzan said.

I whimpered as I could feel his hot breath on my pussy. Before I could lose my nerve, I pushed on his shoulder.

"You have to give me some space, Tarzan."

He nodded and backed up a bit. I hooked my fingers underneath my panties and pulled them off in one movement. Before I could drop it on the ground, Tarzan grabbed the fabric and pulled it to his face. He inhaled my scent, and then, while I watched, he licked the wet patch that my juices had created. A garbled sound came out of my mouth, and he looked up.

"I can't believe you just did that. That's so... naughty," I whispered.

"I love your smell, and I wanted to know if I loved your taste as well," Tarzan said.

A whimper escaped me, as he licked it again. "And do you?"

Seeing my response to his actions, he licked it again, more slowly, before nodding.

"I want to taste more of you," Tarzan growled, and inched closer again, his gaze focused on my wet pussy that was spread open for him to feast his eyes on. "Can I, Jane?" he asked.

I whimpered and nodded, gripping the tree for support.

"Say it," he said as he inched closer to my pussy. His hot breath fanned over my wet pussy, but he didn't lick it. His eyes focused on my face as he said, "Say that I can taste you, Jane." Before I could reply, Tarzan continued, "Say that I can pleasure you with my tongue, my fingers, and my cock."

"Yes," I said, as a shiver of desire coursed through me. "You can do all those things to me. Please."

Before the last word had left my mouth, his mouth focused on my pussy. He licked me from back to front in one swipe with his tongue.

Tarzan groaned, "Even better."

I moaned in response as he devoured my pussy with eager licks. What he lacked in experience he more than made up with enthusiasm.

"Show me how to pleasure you," he said in between licks.

He was already doing an outstanding job, but he hadn't discovered my clit yet. A little nudge in the right direction would only be beneficial for me. I spread open my pussy lips and pointed out the little hidden button.

"This is my clit," I said, and he immediately licked it with such enthusiasm that I squeaked, and pushed him back. "Very sensitive. But oh so pleasurable if touched right."

I showed him how I rubbed around it, occasionally flicking over it with alternating motions. As soon as he understood, he pushed my hand back, studying it with great care. He rubbed it the same way I had, looking at me for responses. I couldn't hold my moans of pleasure back as he touched me.

Tarzan took learning to pleasure me, as seriously as he had every other lesson we had. Every sound I made, every involuntary twitch of my body got his attention and was cataloged somewhere in that brilliant mind of his.

It didn't take long for the pleasure to consume my senses. My moans became louder and more frequent as I felt the pleasure rise inside of me.

"I'm going to come," I moaned as I gripped his hair, holding him in place.

Tarzan lifted his head up, and I felt my climax fizzle out. "Come where?" he asked with his head cocked to the side.

"It's an expression," I huffed out, annoyed. "When you reach the top of your pleasure, you come, or climax, or orgasm."

"Will you come, climax, or orgasm for me, Jane?" Tarzan asked.

Before I could answer, he resumed his ministrations of my pussy and focused on my clit. The pleasure that had started to rise immediately leaped up again and I could feel it crests its climax. With a hoarse cry of pleasure that cascaded through the jungle, I came.

Birds jumped up from their hiding places and chirped in response as waves of pleasure washed over me. I forgot about my surroundings, only experiencing the pleasure that Tarzan was giving me. My body trembled as my muscles clenched and even more wetness came out of me. Tarzan kept on lapping up every drop, only elongating my pleasure. When I was too sensitive, I pushed him away and dropped down against the tree.

He came closer, leaning over me. "I want to do that again," Tarzan said in that deliciously deep voice of his.

I smiled and touched his cheek. "Give me a moment to catch my breath," I said with a voice hoarse from screaming.

"I'll get you water," Tarzan said and disappeared.

His departure felt sudden, and I covered myself up with my skirt. A shiver went through me as the sounds of the Jungle came back in tenfold. I'd never been alone in the Jungle, and without Tarzan's comforting presence, it felt way more dangerous.

When he dove back up the tree, I was almost crying. I jumped up, rushed to him, and started beating my fists against his chest.

"You don't just leave a girl in a tree in the middle of the Jungle after you gave her the most toe-curling orgasm of her life."

"The orgasm was toe-curling?" Tarzan asked, looking down at my feet.

Of course, he focused on the good part of my rant. He gripped my hands and pulled me into an embrace before I could hit him again.

"I brought you water because you sounded like you needed it," he said and gave me a jug from the camp.

I was parched, and it was a sweet gesture, but he couldn't just leave me.

"What I needed after an orgasm like that, is you holding me, kissing me, and not just running off? What if you didn't come back because you got what you wanted?" I said, exposing my insecurities.

Tarzan cupped my cheek, tilting my head up so he could look into my eyes. "I will never stop wanting you, Jane."

"Good," I said, my voice a mere whisper. "Because I'll never stop wanting you to."

I pulled his head down and kissed him. My own taste lingered on his lips, mixed in with his unique, earthy aroma. After a moment of stiffness, he relaxed into the kiss, mimicking my movements. When I opened my mouth, he opened his and our tongues met in a dance of passion that took my breath away.

After both having orgasmed in each other's presence, this kiss somehow felt more intimate. Our bodies touched as our arms intertwined and our breaths intermingled. The stress and anxiety I had from being left alone melted away with each swipe of his tongue and nip of his teeth. For a man who had just learned to pleasure a woman mere hours ago, he certainly knew how to kiss the socks of someone.

I pulled back to be able to breathe again, and his mouth never ceased his assault on me. He kissed a path over my cheek, to my neck, nibbling on every spot he encountered. My legs gave way as Tarzan tasted every inch of me. He caught me in his strong arms and gently laid me down on the trunk. I gazed at the leaves above as his mouth and tongue discovered the rest of my body. He ripped open my shirt to be able to reach my breasts. My cry of protest immediately turned into one of pleasure as he sucked on my nipples. He cupped my breasts, studying them, fascinated.

"You have such big breasts, Jane. So much bigger than any animal I have ever seen."

I blushed as I tried to push his hands away, but he wouldn't release his grip on them.

"They're quite average size for a human."

"They are perfect," Tarzan murmured as he swiped his tongue over my nipples. "They are yours, and every inch of you is perfect, Jane."

I sighed with pleasure, as he continued his path downwards, pulling my skirt off me. Suddenly a shyness crept over me, laying naked for this magnificent, muscular man. Before it could consume my mind, Tarzan threw his head back and bellowed out his Jungle cry.

Startled, I tried to get up, but he immediately covered my body with his, kissing me again.

When his mouth left mine, I asked, "What was that for?"

"To let everyone know that you are mine, Jane."

"Oh, am I now?" I asked, an eyebrow raised.

A gorgeous grin crossed his face as Tarzan pushed his cock against my soaking wet pussy.

"I will claim you as mine, and will fight anyone that wants to stake a claim on you."

His savage words shouldn't arouse me as much as they did, but I loved belonging to someone in an all-consuming way. Tarzan did everything in life with absolute determination, and it seemed that having sex was no different. I had no words to reply, so I just nodded as I pulled him down on me for another kiss.

His mouth distracted me as he pushed his cock closer to me. With a hard thrust, he suddenly breached my entrance, and I cried out from the intrusion and a sharp shot of pain.

He looked at me with a startled look. "Did I hurt you?" Tarzan asked.

I shook my head, but could barely contain the wince as he moved.

"I did," Tarzan said as he started to pull out.

I grasped his shoulder and put my legs around his hips, keeping him close to me. "No, it is normal that it hurts a bit for the first time. I was a virgin."

Tarzan shook his head, his eyes wild with panic and remorse. "It didn't hurt me."

Gripping his head in both my hands, I focused his gaze on me. "Relax," I said in a soothing voice. "If you move again, it will feel good for me."

After a moment of hesitation, he slowly pulled out of me and pushed back in. The friction made pleasure start to rise that overtook any lingering trace of pain.

My body relaxed as I moaned softly. His piercing eyes kept focusing on my face, as he repeated the movement.

"This feels really good, Tarzan. You can go a bit faster," I said.

As soon as he had confirmed that it felt good for me too, he growled and started thrusting into me at a growing pace as he had when he pleasured himself. I could feel the pleasure inside of me rise with every thrust. The sounds that left my mouth were incoherent and filled with pleasure.

"You feel amazing, Jane," he grunted as he fucked me with fierce determination.

"You too," I moaned in response.

I closed my eyes when the pleasure became too much for me, but Tarzan growled. "Look at me. I want to see your pleasure, as I can feel mine."

With a whimper, I opened my eyes and looked into his piercing eyes. Each thrust elicited a moan from me, and I could see it stoke the fire inside of him. Pleasure was rising fast inside of me, but I wasn't there yet.

"Will you come, climax, or orgasm for me, Jane?" Tarzan asked in that focused tone of his.

I nodded, as I pushed my hand between us. He pulled up a bit to give me room to stroke my clit. A few flicks and another round of thrusts were enough to make me come. The pleasure inside of me burst, and it filled my every sense. I could feel my muscles squeeze around him as I cried out my pleasure. Tarzan cried out as well, as he came after a few more thrusts, filling me with his seed.

My body trembled as his shook. Tarzan pulled out, and let him fall down next to me, pulling me close to him in a sweaty and breathless embrace. I basked in my after pleasure as he gently stroked my hair.

"I will never stop wanting you, Jane," he said in an uncharacteristically serious voice.

I looked up at him, seeing him study the leaves above us. "I don't think I can ever let you go," Tarzan said looking down at me.

"I don't think I want you to," I said and kissed him.

It was clear that he was mine, and I was his, forever.

—⁂—

THE END

Rumpelstiltskin

What if the Miller's daughter couldn't give away her firstborn to Rumpelstiltskin because it was already his?

I HAVE ALWAYS BEEN able to read people's thoughts. I used to think it was a gift, but I have since then learned it to be a curse a witch put on my father for not wanting to marry her. As the firstborn, I must carry this burden and try to help my family in any way I could. Everyone spoke of my beauty but whispered about my abilities. Alas, the rumors of my so-called 'powers' reached our king, and he had taken me captive.

"You must give me my deepest desire by a fortnight or you and your entire family will be beheaded," the King said.

There was no use in trying to protest. His mind was filled with his riches and greatness. The King already had everything he could desire, every earthy object that could be bought was in his possession, but yet he wanted more. It was hard to pinpoint what he wanted. He just needed something new, something no one else had and would make him the richest of the lands.

He left me behind in the prison tower in a large, round room filled with straw, a desk, papers, and writing utensils. Anything I needed was at my disposal, but I didn't know what he wanted me to do with them. I tried making a list of anything I could give him, but I came up blank.

"What to give a man that already has everything?" I looked up to the high-pointed ceiling of the tower and spoke to myself. "If just anyone, anyone, anyone could help me."

"Did you call me, dearie?"

A high-pitched voice sounded from above me, and as I gazed up into the dark, I could make out two shiny eyes. The figure suddenly dropped and stood in front of me. He was the oddest-looking man I had ever seen, not very tall, about my size. His skin was a green-golden tint that shimmered in the candlelight, while his eyes were pitch black. A pointy hat adorned his head and finely tailored clothes that had that same shimmer of gold to them, fitted nicely around his form.

"Who are you?" I asked.

Rumpelstiltskin, but I will not tell you that, my dear. I could hear his thoughts, but before I could tell him, he had opened his mouth and I could see sharp teeth gleaming in the flicker of the candlelight.

"I am the one that comes when called three times. I am the one person who could help you. At a price, of course."

I nodded, finally seeing some light at the end of the tunnel, even though in the form of a strange man, I was happy to grasp at any straw of hope.

"Yes, of course, anything at all."

Rumpelstiltskin cocked his head and looked at me with a calculating gaze. His thoughts were scrambled as he went over what he could ask of me, what price I could give him. It was hard to pinpoint until his black eyes focused on my lips.

Suddenly, my mouth felt dry, and I licked my lips to relieve the parched feeling. His eyes glimmered with lust and I could hear his thought focus on the movement of my tongue. He imagined the feel and taste of my lips, as he had never been kissed before. A tingle went through me, nestling just above my pussy as my nipples hardened, and I almost suggested it myself, when he spoke.

"The price will be a kiss from you."

Without hesitation, I agreed. "Yes. But what will we present the king with?"

Rumpelstiltskin smiled as he stalked closer, his sharp teeth gleaming in the dark. His thread was so light it almost seemed as if he was floating over the straw across the room, closer to me. He lifted my chin with a finger, tilting it just a smidge so our mouths were level. I couldn't see the finger, but I felt a sharp prick, almost as if he had claws instead of fingers. The feeling made another shiver wash over me, and arousal fill me.

"Don't you worry that pretty little head of yours. I will make sure the King is satisfied with what we will give him. But first, the matter of the payment. I always demand payment upfront."

"Of course," I whispered, as our lips were only a hair apart.

I could feel his warm breath on my lips, and could almost taste him already. His smell was earthy, green, almost like the deepest corner of the woods, where the light didn't reach, but life still grew.

I wanted to kiss him as well. Many men had tried to seduce me into kisses, but I had always known their thoughts and intentions weren't pure. As dark as this strange man's eyes were, his thoughts were honest and open. Rumpelstiltskin marveled at the softness of my skin as his eyes took in every detail of my face. It felt strange to be admired so openly without him realizing I could hear it all.

As he moved closer so our lips touched, his thoughts turned darker, dirtier, and more intimate. His lips touched mine in the softest of caresses, and I thought he would pull back, but suddenly he deepened the kiss. He grabbed my face so I couldn't move as his other hand encompassed my hip. His claws pricked my skin, causing shivers to wash over my body. He pulled me flush against his body and I gasped at the contact. Rumpelstiltskin didn't waste a second to use the granted access and plundered my mouth with his tongue. His tongue felt strangely textured in a way I couldn't quite understand. It was almost as if he had scales or ridges on his tongue. When he slicked it over mine, I almost moaned at the contact.

I grasped his shoulders to be able to stay upright as the kiss went on and on. His lips moved over mine, as his tongue discovered the intimate places in my mouth. After a moment I became bold and answered the kiss with the same intensity. I touched his sharp teeth with my tongue, loving the hint of pain that accompanied the pleasure of the kiss. My tongue played with his, and he groaned into my mouth. I could feel it vibrate through me as his grip tightened on my hip.

His whole body touched mine, and I could feel something starting to rise between his legs. I moaned as it rubbed me over my pussy and nerve endings came alive that had been dormant for so long. This was my first kiss, my first touch by a man, and I could feel how my body reacted to it all. It felt like Rumpelstiltskin was made for me, and I finally felt safe. I could barely hear his thoughts, just picking up his emotions that reflected my inner turmoil.

My body reacted to his, and I could feel pleasure starting to rise at the onslaught of sensations. His mouth on mine, and his body against mine awoke something inside of me that craved more.

I didn't want this kiss to ever end, but after what felt like an eternity, slowly he backed up. First, he broke the connection between our bodies, until only our lips touched. His warmth left me, and my body trembled with the loss. I desperately wanted to keep his lips, but he pulled his head back. I followed his mouth for a moment before I let go with a sigh.

We stood apart, our eyes fixed on each other. Tension filled the air, but then with a cough, Rumpelstiltskin turned away. "Let's get to work to give the King what he wants."

Dazed, I looked around and realized I was still in the tower, and not somewhere in the woods with him. I had lost track of time, and of where I was during the kiss, and it took me a moment to get my bearings. The King, yes, I needed to give him what he desired or he would kill everyone I loved. I nodded and pulled my arms around me, suddenly feeling cold without his body heat surrounding me.

"Yes, of course. Tell me what I need to do."

"Can you weave?" Rumpelstiltskin asked.

"Sure," I shrugged.

We had some sheep at the farm, and we used the wool to create our winter garments. A shiver went through me as I imagined the warmth of my favorite winter cloak. His eyes focused on me, and with a flick of his hand, I was surrounded by a warm garment. I blinked, as my brain tried to understand what had happened. Magic existed, of course. I was living proof of that, but seeing it with my own eyes was something else entirely. He ignored my inner turmoil and just turned around, looking at all the straws.

"Perfect. I'll spin and you can ."

"Weave what?" I asked, pulling the cloak closer around me, noticing it smelled like him, and a feeling of comfort filled me.

"Ah, but gold, of course, my dear," he said and produced a spinning wheel out of thin air. "I can make gold thread from straw."

My head almost spun. "You can..."

Rumpelstiltskin nodded almost impatiently. "Yes, I can create gold. You'll weave the King a tunic out of the thread and he will have a one-of-a-kind garment that no one else can ever have."

When I didn't respond, he sat down and started to work. It was only when I could see the gold thread appear with my own eyes that I actually believed him.

He was spinning gold from straw, and the room was filled with it. It would be something the King didn't expect, so I sat down next to him to start weaving.

Rumpelstiltskin spent the full four days with me, spinning, helping me, and talking. He only disappeared when the guards came to give me food. Each time they asked me what I would present to the King, and each time I answered that I didn't know yet. The bigger the surprise, the more likely he would let me go, I hoped.

I was grateful for Rumpelstiltskin's help and companionship. His cloak kept me warm during the cold nights, and his voice entertained me during the endless hours of spinning and weaving. He was a rather remarkable man. Almost all his thoughts were genuine, and he spoke all of them out loud. The only time his thoughts and his words didn't agree with each other was when I asked him about the kiss.

"It was my first time," I said as my hands worked to create the fabric from the thread he supplied me with.

"First time?" he asked.

"Yes, I have never been kissed before, so I hope I did it right."

His whole body froze, and the spinning wheel screeched to a halt. First kiss, virgin, with me, amazing, beautiful. His thoughts jumbled around and it felt like his head was too small to encompass it all.

He cleared his throat as he started up the spinning wheel again. "You did alright, my dear."

"Did you enjoy it?" I asked when the silence between us stretched.

More than anything in the entire world. His thoughts made excitement course through me, but when I tried to get him to answer me, he changed the subject. Every time I tried to bring it up again, he diverted and we talked about something else.

When my time was up, we produced the most beautiful garment together. It shimmered in the light and looked as if angels created it. Rumpelstiltskin looked at me with a smile that didn't reach his eyes. He would miss me, but he hoped that I would be happy with what we had created.

"Thank you," I said and grabbed his hand, enjoying the almost scaly feel of his skin. "Without you, I would have never been able to make this."

"It was worth the price," he said as he looked at my lips.

I wanted to ask for another kiss or offer it as thanks, but before I could, the door opened. He disappeared just as the King entered. The King exclaimed his pleasure at the one-of-a-kind tunic, but as the King was a greedy man, he wanted more. He locked me up in the tower again, saying I would need to create a similar garment for his most prized horse so he could prance around the kingdom adorned in gold.

When I was alone again, I looked up at the roof, hoping Rumpelstiltskin would come back. "If just anyone, anyone, anyone could help me, again."

To my great relief, he appeared again. "A greater task will mean a greater price," he said.

I nodded and stepped close to him, already offering my mouth. "Yes, anything at all."

He touched my chin again, letting his thumb run along my lower lip. His thoughts were a jumble of every possible scenario he wanted to act out. Each and everyone was erotic, and intriguing in nature. Whatever he would suggest, I would accept. Not out of fear for my family, but out of a desire for this man that I had grown to care for in the past fortnight.

"I want more than a mere kiss. I want a night of pleasure with you."

A smile curved my lips, and I pushed my tongue out to lick at his thumb. His earthy taste filled my mouth, and I could feel the intriguing texture on my tongue. His breathing stuttered and the desire in his mind grew.

"Yes," I said.

Before I could say another word, he pulled me into his embrace and kissed me again. I had been craving his lips since our first kiss, and it was even better than I remembered. This time, he didn't hesitate to plunder my mouth. His movements were urgent as if he feared I would change my mind. I wouldn't. I wanted him as much as he wanted me. His textured tongue met mine in a dance of lust, and I moaned at the thought of what that would feel like between my legs.

Rumpelstiltskin pushed me down in the fresh straw as his hands roamed my body. In an instant, my clothes were gone and I lay naked before his greedy eyes. He looked at me as if I was more precious than all the gold in the world. With a flick of his hand, his own garments disappeared as well, and I could see him in all his glory. His whole body was covered in some type of scales that shimmered in the candlelight.

I let my eyes wander over his naked form until they arrived at his cock. I gasped, looking at the ever-growing appendage. It looked massive and frightening as it cast a dark shadow over me. Excitement filled me, and I could already feel my body respond to prepare for our joining. My nipples puckered, desire nestled deep inside of me, and my pussy produced wetness.

Looking at his cock, I wanted to touch him, taste him, and feel him inside of me. It seemed the same texture I had felt on his tongue, also covered his cock. The scales created a ridged pattern that had to feel heavenly inside of me. I stretched out my hand to grasp him, but he stopped me before I could touch him.

"I don't want this night to end yet, my dear," he said as he lightly kissed the palm of my hand to soften the rejection.

"Me neither," I said in a husky tone that didn't sound like me.

My heart was beating a thousand miles a minute and my voice sounded rough and wanton. I've never wanted anything as much as I wanted Rumpelstiltskin, and I knew he felt exactly the same.

"I want to taste every inch of you, caress every part, and make you come more times than you can count before I even enter you," he said.

My breathing stuttered, and I didn't know what to answer. I wanted all of it and more, but I also wanted to touch him. Rumpelstiltskin didn't give me a chance to respond as he pushed my legs open and descended between them. He breathed in my scent and exclaimed his delight in a raspy voice.

His sharp claws held my legs firmly in place as his tongue pushed between my pussy lips. The texture felt magnified a thousand times on my pussy than it had in my mouth. It was almost as if he was made for pleasure, and all I could do was let the experience take me higher and higher. I moaned and trashed as pleasure as I had never felt before washed over me. The feeling of his tongue created the most delicious friction as he devoured me with relish. He discovered every pleasure spot between my pussy lips with it as if he was determined to memorize it to heart.

The indescribable pleasure was mixed with small tinges of pain as his claws scraped over my skin when I moved too wildly. Sounds came out of me that I didn't recognize and had never made before. I could feel the pleasure inside of me build with each touch, sweep, and lick of his tongue. He never even touched any other part of my body, but it was enough to make me crash off the steepest cliff.

The slightest nick of his teeth over my clit made my body tremble, and the pleasure inside of me burst. Waves of pleasure washed over me as I cried out gibberish. I didn't know if I wanted him to continue or stop, as pleasure filled my every sense.

I might have passed out for a second because as my body was coming down from its high, I was suddenly surrounded by his arms. I lay in his embrace as his hands caressed my trembling body.

"That was only the beginning, my dear. I have all night with you."

I snuggled closer to him, gently caressing his scaly skin, playing with the flicker of gold that seemed to dance over him.

"What if I want more?" I asked in a soft voice.

His body stiffened, and his hands stilled. Immediately, I missed the comforting rhythm he had played over my skin. After a moment where I could feel his thoughts shoot out in all directions, he resumed his soothing touches.

"I'll give you everything you want for as long as our deal stands," he said.

I wanted to ask what would happen after, but he lifted my head and took my mouth in another passionate kiss. No more words were exchanged as he kissed, licked, and caressed every inch of my body. He marveled at the softness of my skin but seemed afraid to voice it out loud. Every time I tried to talk, he silenced me with a kiss. He didn't believe that I could want more of him than what I had bargained for.

After my umpteenth orgasm, he positioned himself between my legs. His rock-hard cock was covered in precum and slid easily between my soaking wet pussy lips. I moaned, unable to utter any other word than yes, when he slowly entered me. My wetness and many orgasms eased the way for his impressive cock to fill me. Each ridge created sparks of pleasure that felt like mini orgasms. It felt like he went on forever, stuffing me full with his cock, until I almost felt like bursting, and he finally bottomed out.

"You feel amazing, my dear," Rumpelstiltskin groaned in my ear as his body trembled.

"Yes, please, move," I begged.

Another shiver racked his body as I voiced my request, but he obeyed, unable to do anything but that. He pulled back slowly, each ridge eliciting a gasp from me as it exited me. When he pushed back in, all the breath left my lungs and pleasure filled me. My muscles squeezed around him, making him groan in pleasure, and breaking his composure. He grabbed my hips and started thrusting inside me without control.

Rumpelstiltskin fucked me hard in the straw, making me come over and over again. I didn't even know where one orgasm ended and the other began. I floated around on a cloud of pleasure, as he finally took his own pleasure as well. It didn't take long before his cock throbbed inside of me, and he filled me with his cum. His guttural cry cascaded across the room and filled me with joy, and pleasure.

He pulled out and dropped down beside me, pulling me into his arms again. Too well pleasured and tired to talk, I nuzzled close to him and let my eyes rest for a moment.

When I woke up, he was on the other side of the room, working on his spinning wheel. As I opened my mouth to greet him, the lock of the door sounded through the room. Rumpelstiltskin looked at me, waved with his hand to dress me, and disappeared.

When I had received my breakfast, had eaten, and drank, I called out to him again. Rumpelstiltskin appeared and worked on the spinning wheel again. I wished I could pull him back in the straw, and just forget about the King, but I couldn't let my family die for my own selfish reasons.

We spent the rest of the week working and sleeping together. Each time when the sun dropped, and I got tired, he tried to resist me, but I wouldn't let him. I craved his touch, and his nearness, getting addicted to him in such a short time.

I discovered that he was an imp that traveled around and traded favors with people. His skill to turn straw into gold was perfect for any kind of deal. Usually, he dealt in material favors, like jewelry or land, but with me, he had wanted something more.

I didn't know what was so different about me that made him make this kind of deal with me, but I embraced it with both hands. I didn't want this week to end. In our little bubble, we were happy together, and I knew it would be over as soon as the King returned again. I tried to convince him to stay, but as soon as the week was over, and we had created another unique garment for the King, he disappeared again.

The King was yet again not satisfied with what I had offered him. He always wanted more, but I refused to give it to him. After a lot of back and forth, we agreed to one last deal. I got one month to create a golden tapestry to hang behind his throne that depicted his greatest victories. Yet again he locked me in the tower with fresh straw, and I called out to Rumpelstiltskin.

Before the last word had left my mouth, he already stood before me. He kissed me with so much passion and emotion that I almost couldn't speak.

"What deal to make this time, my dear," Rumpelstiltskin murmured as he gently stroked my cheek. I leaned into the touch, having missed him even for the few moments we had been apart. "You have already given me so much already. You have made me the happiest imp alive for these past two weeks."

"I'll give you anything you wish for," I said.

Suddenly, his thoughts turned clear and I could see his deepest desire; a family of his own. A child, and a wife. Me. I could feel his thoughts turn around and around, trying to figure out something else I could give him, but he always came back to that image. He never imagined having a child at all, but he could make a deal out of it.

"Are you willing to accept the trade even though the payment will be done after the deal?"

"Yes, tell me what you want from me," I said with a smile.

Joy filled me with the thought of having him as my husband and creating a life between us. Doubt crept into his mind as he looked at me, realizing I was far too beautiful to ever be able to love a monster like him. I stepped closer, hugging him, trying to comfort him without words, but he took a step back.

"I want your firstborn."

"But, we could..."

Rumpelstiltskin put a finger on my lips, cutting off my words. "This is what I have chosen for a price. You must give me your firstborn. Only then will our score be settled. If you refuse, I leave now and the king will not be pleased."

Tears pricked in my eyes as I realized I had to accept the deal. I couldn't refuse, but it could win me some time. We had a month together to create the garment, and I would make sure to have him in my bed every night.

"I accept," I whispered, my voice not strong enough to be spoken aloud.

Rumpelstiltskin smiled, and I could feel his relief. He knew he couldn't have me, but he rejoiced in the fact that he could have a part of me, and never be alone again.

"We have a month together," I said, hoping it to be enough to make him realize my feelings for him were as strong as his for me. "Please come to bed with me each night. I sleep better with you next to me."

There wasn't enough gold in the world to make him refuse me. Before he could grab me and distract me with all the pleasure he could give me, I put up my hand. "I want to make you a deal."

"I can never refuse a good deal," he said as he slowly approached me like a predator ready to devour its prey.

"I want to taste you," I said.

Rumpelstiltskin halted his nearing and cocked his head. He tried to figure out why, and what I would get out of this deal. When he couldn't think of a single reason why I would want to give him pleasure, my heart almost broke. He might look monstrous and make deals in exchange for favors, but he was also an honorable man who had shown me nothing but compassion and pleasure in the short while I had met him.

"Please, just give me this," I said.

Rumpelstiltskin was unable to refuse my pleading gaze and nodded in acceptance. With a flick of his hand, we were both naked. I knelt before him, reaching for his hardening cock. When I grasped him, he growled. Looking up, I could see his face contorted in pleasure, his eyes fiery with passion. Not breaking his gaze, I stuck out my tongue to flick it over his head. His earthy taste filled my senses, and I moaned in pleasure. His breath wheezed out, as his whole body trembled.

"Don't play with me, my dear, or you might get more than you bargained for."

"Don't hold back," I said as I focused back on his cock.

The unique texture of his cock fascinated me as I studied every inch of it. It almost looked like he had scales, but in such a small and dense way that they created ridges circling around his cock. The drop of precum oozing out of the tip shone like gold in the candlelight. I flicked out my tongue again to catch it before it dropped down. Another growl sounded from above me, and with a smile, I looked up.

Rumpelstiltskin gnashed his teeth together, to try to keep from saying something he would regret. He never imagined someone as beautiful as me would ever do something like this for him. I wanted to tell him that I loved every second of it, but he would never believe my words.

I had to show him my feelings with actions, so I gripped him tight and pulled him further into my mouth. Ridge after ridge passed my lips until I only had half of him inside of me. I gagged but tried to take more of him. The feeling of him in my mouth, and knowing that I was the reason that this amazing male was trembling made my arousal shoot up. I moaned around his cock, as wetness gathered between my legs, and the smell of arousal filled the air.

His whole body trembled as his control snapped. Rumpelstiltskin grasped my head and thrust in my mouth, taking his own pleasure from me. I tried to open as wide as I could to give him easy access and suppressed my natural instincts to fight. It only took a few thrusts before his cock throbbed and I could feel his cum fill my throat. I swallowed every drop and gently cleaned his cock with my tongue when he pulled back.

To my amazement, he hadn't diminished in hardness. Rumpelstiltskin pulled me up, pushed me against the wall, and entered me in one thrust. I moaned as he filled me, each ridge sparking pleasure inside of me. Holding one hand securely at my hip, as the other braced the wall, he started fucking me hard. I could do nothing but enjoy the ride and exclaim my pleasure loudly with each thrust.

The pleasure inside of me grew as he fucked me against the wall. His ridges created the most amazing sensation with each pull and push, stimulating my clit with every move. I didn't mind the cold wall against my back, or his unforgiving grip on my hip that would surely leave a bruise. I loved that he lost control, and took me in any way he could.

Rumpelstiltskin bends his one knee slightly, changing the angle just enough to push at a spot inside of me that made me see stars. I screamed like a banshee when the most sudden orgasm rushed over me. Waves of pleasure filled me as I squeezed his cock with my pussy muscles. He growled but didn't come with me. As soon as my orgasm was over, he pulled out of me, pushed my face down on the ground in the straw, and entered me from behind.

"I'm not done with you yet, my dear," Rumpelstiltskin said as he fucked me with all his might.

I was a moaning mess of pleasure as he played my body as his own personal instrument. He made me make sounds I had never heard before and showed me ways of pleasure I never even imagined. He took me in any way possible, until I fell asleep in his arms, with his cock still buried deep inside of me.

After that night, we fell into a comfortable routine. My feelings for him grew, but each time I tried to tell him and convince him of my love for him, he disappeared, only appearing again when I was out of yarn for the tapestry. After a while, I gave up talking and tried to show him each night how much he meant to me. I knew he loved me, and I could hear it in his thoughts each day, but he couldn't believe that someone as beautiful as me could love someone as hideous as him. It didn't matter that I kissed every inch of him, that I told him I loved him during the throes of my orgasm, or that I didn't want to let him go after our lovemaking.

Time passed, and before I knew it, the King was at my door again and Rumpelstiltskin was gone. Finally, the King was pleased with what I had done and let me go back to my village. My family was happy to see me. They had fared rather well during my time away as a bag of gold had appeared on their doorstep each day I had been gone. I missed Rumpelstiltskin greatly, but every time I tried to call him, he didn't appear. The only spark of joy in my life was the discovery that I was with child, and I knew that I would see him again.

Months later, when I gave birth to my child, Rumpelstiltskin came to collect his debt.

"I cannot give him to you," I said, holding my little bundle of joy in my arms.

"Why not? You cannot break our deal," Rumpelstiltskin said, his voice trembling.

"I cannot give you something that is already yours," I said as pulled the fabric away from the face of our son.

His skin had the same golden tone as his father, and combined with the blue from my eyes, he looked like an angel.

"Mine?" Rumpelstiltskin said with wonder in his voice as he stepped closer.

I grabbed his hand so he couldn't disappear again. "How can we break our deal? How can we be together? Please, there must be a way."

He shook his head, still staring at our son until a thought appeared in his mind. Perhaps? But no, it isn't possible... I could never.

I squeezed his hand, pulling his gaze to me. "Any way at all, please."

"The only way for a deal with me to be broken is if you can guess my true name, and I cannot give it to you knowingly."

A wave of relief washed over me as a laugh escaped me. It would be that easy? I had known his name for as long as I had known him, but I never thought to speak it out loud, as it was such a mouthful. His brow furrowed as he looked at me.

"Why are you laughing, my dear? It is not an easy task to guess my real name."

I smiled up at him and cupped his cheek, reveling in the all-too-familiar feel of his textured skin. "But I've known your name for all this time, my love. It's Rumpelstiltskin."

His eyes widened with shock and his mouth opened and closed like a fish. "But... how?" he stuttered.

"I can hear people's thoughts, my love, and I know how much you love me, and how you wished to be with me and become a family. And now we can. I love you," I said.

"I love you too," he said, and he kissed me.

When the baby in my arms made a sound of disagreement, he pulled back. "What's his name?" he asked.

"Rumpel," I said with a smile.

THE END

Authors Note

I am super happy to share the first collection of my new series!

I loved fairytales growing up, and I love imagining all the ways those classic tales can turn smutty. I still have plenty of ideas left, and I hope I'll get to share them with you!

Anyway, I hope you enjoyed the story! Please leave a rating and / or a review if you did!

About the author

Lilith Leana writes what she loves; Monster erotica.

Born and raised in Belgium, she devours ebooks as if it heals her. In her day job she loves to organize, plan and make schedules for other people, but when the night falls she can let loose with her fantasies which star all kinds of Monsters and Human couplings.

YOU CAN ALSO FIND ME on:

Author Home Page: https://lilithleanaauthor.start.page/

Instagram: https://www.instagram.com/lilithleana/

Etsy Shop: https://www.etsy.com/be/shop/SteamyPublishing?coupon=FREESHIPPING2

Or you can email me: lilith.leana666@gmail.com

DEAR READER

If you enjoyed this book, please consider leaving a review. Indie writers depend on reviews to keep writing and publishing.

Thank you so much ❤

Lilith

Also by the author

Series & Collections

Creature Loving Volume 1: A Monster Erotica Collection[1]
Creature Loving Volume 2: A Monster Erotica Collection[2]
Creature Loving Volume 3: A Monster Erotica Collection[3]
My Ghostly Lover[4] - Full story: 3 Parts + Epilogue
Part I: Taken by the Ghost[5]
Part II: Freeing my Ghost[6]
Part III: Saving my Ghost[7]

Fairytale Retelling Short Stories

The Beast[8]
Hook[9]
Frost[10]
The Jungle Man[11]
Rumpelstiltskin[12]

---

1. https://books2read.com/u/47gLkj

2. https://books2read.com/u/47VMwA

3. https://books2read.com/u/bW0pk1

4. https://books2read.com/u/3J6dxJ

5. https://books2read.com/u/3yVerv

6. https://books2read.com/u/mBvKok

7. https://books2read.com/u/bwrZN9

8. https://books2read.com/u/4ENaEA

9. https://books2read.com/u/4Nolg9

10. https://books2read.com/u/mvyGrX

11. https://books2read.com/u/3R0Aqj

Monster Short Stories

Holiday Short Stories

12. https://books2read.com/u/bryN0w

13. https://books2read.com/u/boy8vV

14. https://books2read.com/links/ubl/3kYPzN

15. https://books2read.com/u/md1P5w

16. https://books2read.com/u/b5jJAk

17. https://books2read.com/u/3LVqEX

18. https://books2read.com/u/38PLpB

19. https://books2read.com/u/bQj7VP

20. https://books2read.com/u/m2d8Y6

21. https://books2read.com/u/bON1NE

22. https://books2read.com/u/4ARgJo

23. https://books2read.com/u/bxrZZo

24. https://books2read.com/u/bzKW7Z

25. https://books2read.com/u/bopvPZ

26. https://books2read.com/u/3R0Lgv

27. https://d.docs.live.net/c24c6c9747f7bd15/Bureaublad/Vrije%20tijd/Paranormal/books2read.com/u/

mezO7z

<u>Helping the Green Goblin Steal Christmas</u>[28]
<u>Catching Cupid</u>[29]
<u>Missing St. Patrick's Day</u>[30]

Coming Soon - Someday

The House of Desire: Multiple part Series - Coming Soon - 2023

---

28. https://books2read.com/u/mZEGjR

29. https://books2read.com/u/ml8dvY

30. https://books2read.com/u/mvyO1J

Sneak Peak of my next story:
The Frog Prince

What if the Swan Princess kissed the Frog Prince, and they helped each break their curse?

"What's your name?"

"Odette," I said. I looked up and saw nothing but warmth and honesty in his eyes. He truly wanted to help me. "And yours?"

"Henry."

My eyes widened as a distant memory resurfaced. "You're the crown prince Henry that disappeared when I was younger."

He cocked his head, a sad smile crossing his face. "I guess I am."

"You were next in line for the throne." Another memory popped up. "You can help me," I said with a smile.

"That's amazing! Tell me how," he said excitedly, pulling me closer.

I suddenly became very aware of his very naked body against my thin dress. My nipples hardened, and brushed against his naked chest, as I could feel his cock rise between us. Clearing my throat, I pulled back slightly.

"I'm sorry," Henry said as he stepped back as well. "I didn't mean to..." he covered his cock with his hands, and smiled sheepishly at me. "I haven't been touched in a while, and I was a teenager when... Doesn't matter. How can I help."

I could feel my cheeks heat up, as I tried to tear my gaze from his hands, and what he was hiding behind them. I hadn't been touched in ages as well, and I missed his comforting warmth already.

"Don't worry," I said. "I get it. So you can help me, by uhm." I coughed suddenly aware of what I was going to ask. I took a steadying breath and looked him in the eyes. "By marrying me."

"Oh," Henry said nodding slowly. "I can do that. Is that all that needs to be done to break the curse?"

"Well, not all. I need to wed, and bed a king," I said remembering the words the wizard had spoken to me. "So when you become king, you could... maybe." I shook my head. "I'm sorry, forget about it, I am asking too much from you."

Henry stepped closer, pulling me into his embrace again. I sighed in delight, realizing how touch-starved I had been during the past years. His arms tightened around me, as I hugged him back. Caressing his naked back, my cold hands warmed up for the first time in forever.

"You're not, Odette. Without you, I would have hopped around for how many years to come. Maybe you don't realize, but there aren't a lot of maiden princesses in the forest willing to kiss a frog."

I snorted, "Nor are there kings, willing to marry a swan."

His laugh rumbled through me, making me feel safe and cherished. We stood in each other embrace for a while, taking comfort from one another. We both ignored his erection and just focused on the pleasure of each other nearness.

When the sun rose, I had to let him go. Henry pulled my face slowly to him, giving me every opportunity to refuse. His lips touched mine, in a gentle, loving kiss. It was my first kiss if you didn't count the one in his frog form. A feeling of rightness filled me as his lips moved over mine. I moved with him, deepening the kiss, wishing it could last forever. Too soon I had to step back. As the sunlight touched me, I transformed back into my swan form.

Henry gently patted my head, in the same way I had done when he was a frog.

"I promise I will be back in a month, and we will break this curse together. Don't lose hope yet, Odette, I will help you."

The Frog Prince - Coming Soon - 3 June

Don't miss out!

Visit the website below and you can sign up to receive emails whenever Lilith Leana publishes a new book. There's no charge and no obligation.

https://books2read.com/r/B-A-YTZU-WOBJC

BOOKS2READ

Connecting independent readers to independent writers.